·A Venetian Tale·

POME & PEEL

Retold by AMY EHRLICH
Pictures by LÁSZLÓ GÁL

A Puffin Pied Piper

PUFFIN PIED PIPER BOOKS
Published by the Penguin Group
Penguin Books USA Inc., 375 Hudson Street, New York, New York 10014, U.S.A.
Penguin Books Ltd, 27 Wrights Lane, London W8 5TZ, England
Penguin Books Australia Ltd, Ringwood, Victoria, Australia
Penguin Books Canada Ltd, 10 Alcorn Avenue, Toronto, Ontario, Canada M4V 3B2
Penguin Books (N.Z.) Ltd, 182-190 Wairau Road, Auckland 10, New Zealand
Penguin Books Ltd, Registered Offices: Harmondsworth, Middlesex, England
Originally published in hardcover by Dial Books for Young Readers
A Division of Penguin Books USA Inc.

Text copyright © 1990 by Amy Ehrlich
Pictures copyright © 1990 by László Gál
All rights reserved
Library of Congress Catalog Card Number 88-7140
Printed in Hong Kong by South China Printing Company (1988) Limited
First Puffin Pied Piper Printing 1993
ISBN 0-14-054587-5
1 3 5 7 9 10 8 6 4 2
Designed by Atha Tehon

A Pied Piper Book is a registered trademark of
Dial Books for Young Readers,
a division of Penguin Books USA Inc.,
® TM 1,163,686 and ® TM 1,054,312.

POME & PEEL
is also available in hardcover from
Dial Books for Young Readers.

The full-color artwork was prepared using alkyd colors,
egg tempera, and casein tempera. It was then color-separated
and reproduced as red, blue, yellow, and black halftones.

For Penny Patch and David Martin

A.E.

———————————————————

To Dr. Achim Pfeiffer
with sincere friendship

L.G.

Once there was a husband and wife who had everything they wanted except a child. All their wealth could not help them get one, and it seemed as if they would go into their old age alone. But one day at market the husband met a wizard. "Ah," said the husband, "perhaps you can tell me how my wife might have a child."

"That's easy," the wizard replied. "You must give her this red apple to eat. In nine months the child will be born."

The wife was very happy to hear this news and at once asked her maid to prepare the apple. The girl popped the apple peel into her mouth, then served her mistress the fruit without thinking anymore about it.

But a few months later when the wife's belly began to swell, so did the maid's, and they each felt a strange movement like a little fish swimming inside them. Finally they consulted the husband. "Did you eat the apple peel?" he asked the maid.

"What of it?" she answered.

"Yes, what of it?" said the wife, for she and her maid were good friends.

"You fools!" cried the husband. "Now both of you are pregnant!"

"Don't worry about him," whispered the wife to the maid. "We'll have our children together and raise them as brothers."

It was just as the wife had said. The maid went into labor first and gave birth to a ruddy, dark-haired boy. A half hour later the wife's child was born. He was a boy too, but pale and fair.

As soon as the husband saw them, he became reconciled and loved both children equally. They were called Pome and Peel for the two parts of the apple, and until they were young men they were as carefree and happy as birds in the sky.

But one day the brothers heard about a wizard's daughter from a distant city. She was said to be very beautiful, but she would not appear at her balcony and no one could make her laugh. The brothers had to see her! They begged and pleaded until at last their father agreed.

"Then the metalsmith must make a bronze horse with a hollow belly so that we can hide in it with our mandolins and lutes," said Pome. Peel had imagined this horse too, although he had not told his brother. Such things sometimes happened between them.

The bronze horse was built on wooden wheels and it carried the brothers along until they reached the wizard's palace. So amazed was he at the sight of a horse playing music, that he pulled his daughter out onto her balcony. There she stood, blinking in the sunshine, and she was as beautiful as the moon and stars.

Pome and Peel played a love song and finally the girl looked down at the bronze horse and began to laugh. Then the wizard led the horse into the great entry hall of the palace. "Stay here, my child," he told his daughter. "Stay and listen to the horse's songs."

As soon as he was gone, Pome and Peel jumped from the horse's belly and bowed to the girl. Of course she was frightened, but they reassured her and said they meant her no harm. "Just tell us to leave and we will," Peel said. But the girl would not do it. They were handsome and gallant, and she wanted them to play because she loved music.

For many days the three of them were inseparable, and when it was time for them to return home, the girl said she wanted to go with them. Pome and Peel looked at each other. Then Peel slowly nodded.

Pome said, "If you truly want to come, will you marry me?" The girl agreed at once. She packed her things and jumped into the horse's belly. Then the palace gates swung open and they all rode out.

As soon as the wizard came back, he knew that he had been betrayed. He saw the bronze horse far away in the hills and he put three curses upon his daughter.

"She who so loves horses will find three of them, a white horse, a red one, and a black. But she will ride the white horse, and this one will betray her.

"Next she will find three dogs. She will want to keep the white dog, and this one will betray her.

"And on her wedding night an animal dreadful to look upon will come into the room, and this animal will betray her."

But as the wizard spoke, three witches were passing by and heard every word. They took pity on the girl, who had been careless only once, and they sought her out at the tavern where she was staying with the brothers.

Pome was on one side of the bed and the girl was on the other, but Peel was in the middle and he was only half asleep.

Said the first witch, "He has vowed that his daughter will choose a white horse, but if she rides him, he will betray her. A man who loves her must sever the horse's head or all is lost."

Said the second witch, "He has vowed that she will choose a white dog to keep, but he will betray her. A man who loves her must sever the dog's head or all is lost."

Said the last witch, "He has vowed that on her wedding night a loathesome beast will come into the room and betray her. A man who loves her must sever the beast's head or all is lost."

And then the witches said together, "But woe to him who reveals these curses, for he will turn to stone."

Peel jumped from his bed in terror, but the three witches had disappeared. What was Peel to think? There was nothing to say, nothing yet to be done. He spent a sleepless night, and in the morning they started back on their travels.

They had not gone far when they met a man with three horses, a white one, a red one, and a black. It was just as the witches had said; the girl had to have the white one. But when she tried to mount it, Peel severed the horse's head with his sword.

The girl berated him. He was heartless and cruel, she said. How could he kill an innocent creature?

Pome spoke for his brother then. "I'm certain he did not mean to do it," he told her. "You must forgive him for my sake."

So the wizard's daughter agreed and they continued on their travels. They were near the brothers' courtyard when they met a man with three beautiful little dogs. The girl wanted to have the white one, but just as she was about to take it, Peel cut off its head.

This time the wizard's daughter would not listen to Pome's pleas for his brother. Who knows where their fight would have ended if the mistress, the maid, and the brothers' father had not come running out?

"My sons! My sons!" exclaimed the father while the two women surveyed the girl, each wondering which son she had been promised to. Then Pome took her hand and said, "This is my beloved."

Both mothers went to the kitchen to prepare the wedding feast, and Pome and the wizard's daughter were married that very night with great celebration.

"Do you know what happened?" the girl said afterward. And she told the story of the white horse and the white dog, accusing Peel and saying he must be punished.

They pleaded with her, using the same arguments that Pome had earlier. The girl listened and at last agreed to forgive Peel, as it was her wedding night.

During the meal he had sat silent and thoughtful, saying no word in his own defense. Finally his mother asked if something was wrong. "I am just tired. Please forgive me," said Peel.

Everyone thought he was going to his bed, but instead Peel hid in the wedding chamber. There he lay waiting for the loathesome beast, and his heart pounded.

In the middle of the night he heard the beast creeping slowly toward the bed. Nothing could have stopped Peel then! He leaped up and severed the monster's terrible head with one blow.

But afterward neither the head nor the body could be found anywhere in the room. The bride and bridegroom awoke and saw only Peel, breathing hard with his sword in his hand. "Aha!" the girl cried, "I have forgiven you twice already, but I will not forgive you again." And when she demanded that Peel be hung as a murderer, not even his mother could save him.

The night he was to die Peel asked to speak to the wizard's daughter. It was his last wish and so she came to him.

"Do you remember the tavern we stopped at?" he asked.

"Yes, I do," said she.

"You were sleeping, but three witches came and they said your father had put three curses on you. He vowed that you would find three horses and a white one would betray you. If a man who loved you severed its head, nothing would happen, but woe to him who revealed this curse, for he would be turned to stone."

As Peel spoke, his feet and legs turned into marble.

"Stop, I beg you!" the girl screamed. "Don't say any more!"

"I would die by hanging, but I choose this death instead." Then Peel told her the second curse about the little dogs, and he turned to marble up to his neck.

His throat was turning to marble and he could hardly breathe or talk, but still he had to continue. "And finally your father vowed that on your wedding night a loathesome beast would enter the room. If a man who loved you severed its head, nothing would happen, but woe to him… who revealed this curse… for he… would be… turned to stone."

And there in the prison as the wizard's daughter wrung her hands and wept, Peel turned completely into marble.

"Oh, what have I done? If only I could save him!" she moaned. Suddenly she thought of her father, and she wrote him a letter begging his forgiveness and asking that he come to her.

The wizard, who truly missed his daughter, saddled his fastest horse and arrived the next day. "Ah, Father," she said as she greeted him, "you must have mercy. This statue was once a boy, brother to my husband. He saved me from the curses you gave me and it turned him into stone."

The wizard sighed and said, "For the love I bear you, I will do this as well." Then he took a magical balm and touched it to Peel's forehead.

The boy came to life again, and instead of hanging him they marched through the city while trumpets played and people cried from the road-sides, "Long live Peel! Long live the loyal brother!"